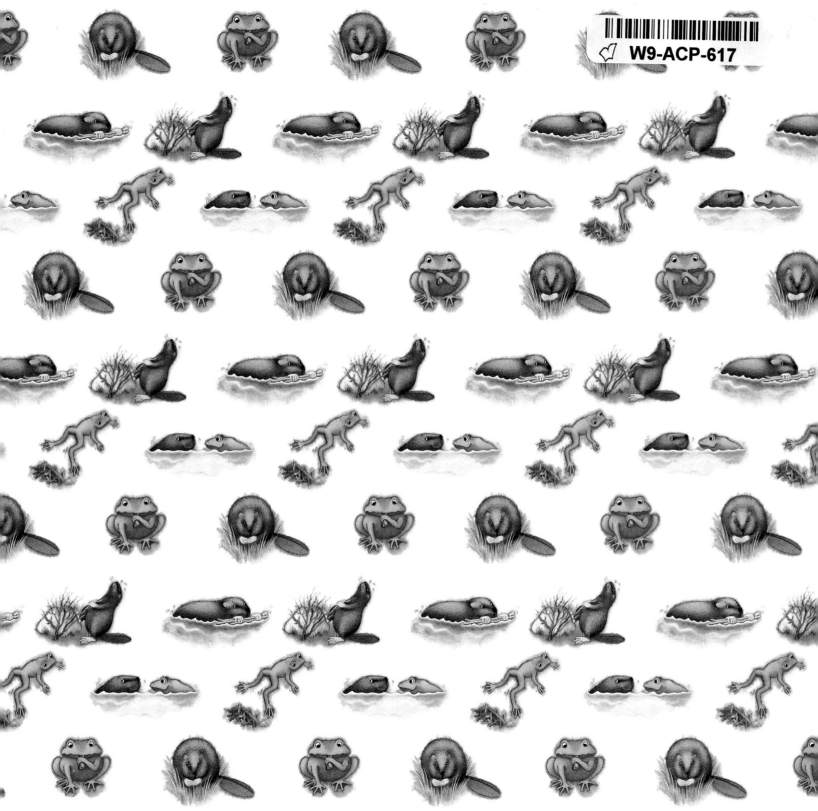

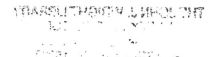

For Yannik Ferenc

1 3 5 7 9 10 8 6 4 2

First published in Great Britain, Canada, Australia and New Zealand
in 1989 by North-South Books, an imprint of Rada Matija AG

British Library Cataloguing in Publication Data

Pfister, Marcus
Boris Beaver
I. Title
833'.914 [J]

ISBN 1-55858-019-0

Marcus Pfister

Boris Beaver

Translated by Anthea Bell

North-South Books
New York

The first rays of the sun shone brightly on the beavers' pond. But Father Beaver, Mother Beaver and their son Boris were already awake.

Mother and Father Beaver had been working busily for weeks, building a dam to make the stream into a pond. Then they built their lodge in the middle of the pond.

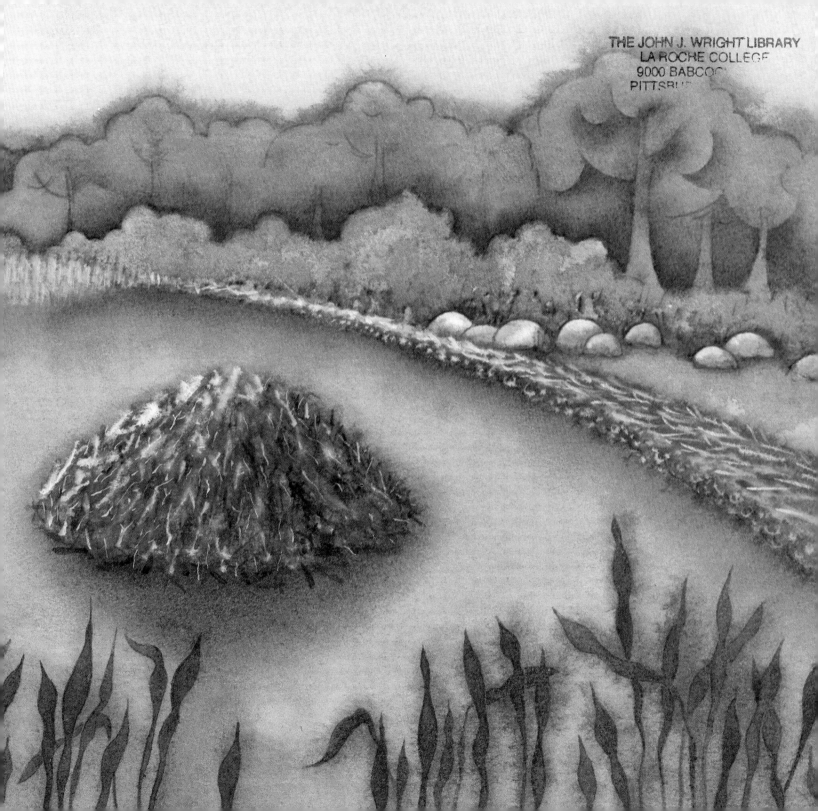

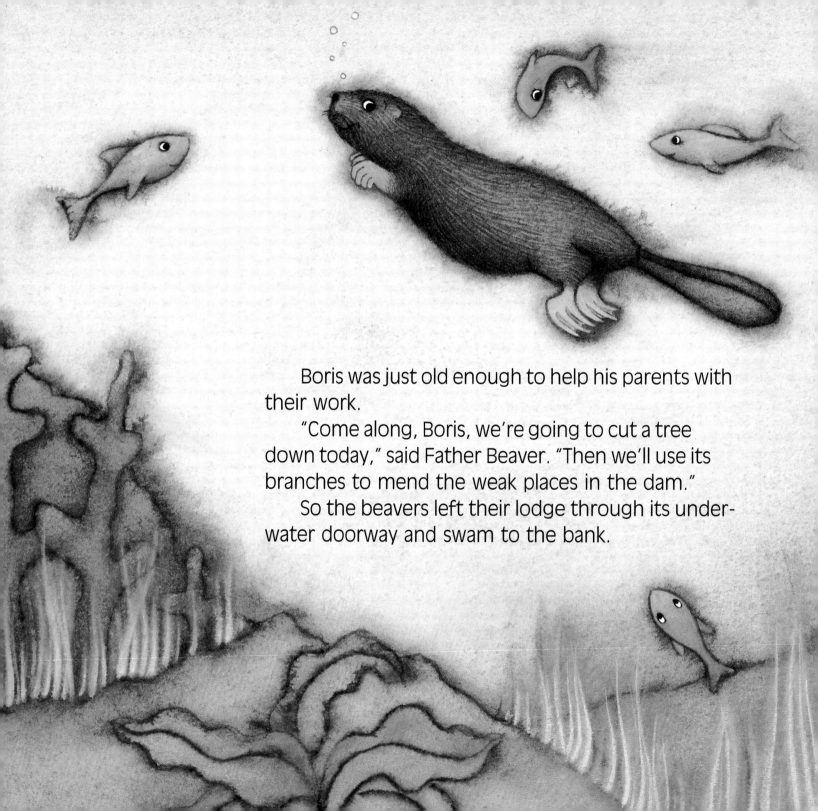

Boris was just old enough to help his parents with their work.

"Come along, Boris, we're going to cut a tree down today," said Father Beaver. "Then we'll use its branches to mend the weak places in the dam."

So the beavers left their lodge through its underwater doorway and swam to the bank.

Father Beaver chose a good tree on the edge of the wood and set to work with his sharp teeth. "You have a go at that bush over there, Boris," he said. "We could use a few more twigs for our lodge."

Boris scuttled eagerly over to the bush and tried pulling it up by the roots. He tugged, and tugged until he was red in the face.

"I'd try my teeth if I were you," Father Beaver advised him, smiling.

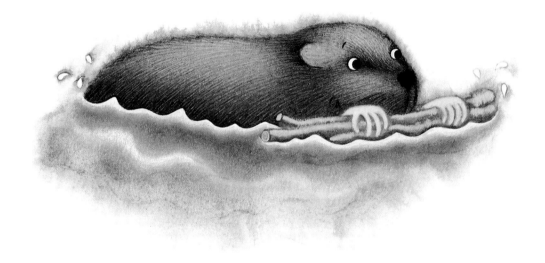

And Boris had very soon gnawed through the branches of the bush. He gathered them together and dragged them to the bank. He swam over to the lodge with his bundle of sticks and added them to the roof. Then he splashed slowly back.

As soon as Boris was in the wood again he heard his father's warning cry. "Watch out, Boris, the tree's falling!"

Boris just had time to jump aside. He was trembling all over. Father Beaver was shaken too. "That was a close thing!" he said. "Go and play until you've recovered from the shock, Boris. We can work on the dam this afternoon."

Back in the cool water, Boris soon forgot his fright. He liked to swim better than anything else in the world. He swam right across the pond, until he suddenly collided with something.

He turned over in surprise. "Who are you?" he asked.

"I'm Freddy Frog. Hey, you're swimming around this pond as if you owned it!"

Boris laughed.

"Well, in a way the pond really does belong to us beavers. After all, we made it by building our dam. Still, I'm sorry I bumped into you. Come on, let's have a game!"

Freddy sat on a floating tree trunk and let Boris push him across the pond.

In the afternoon Freddy went to the dam with Boris. "I don't think I can be much help," he said. "But I always like to watch other people work!"

Mother and Father Beaver had dragged a whole lot of branches from the tree they had felled over to the dam.

"There's a very weak spot there, Boris. Help me get this branch firmly anchored," said his father.

However, just as Boris was going to put the branch in place, the water of the pond burst through the dam. A big jet of water swept Boris down to the bed of the stream.

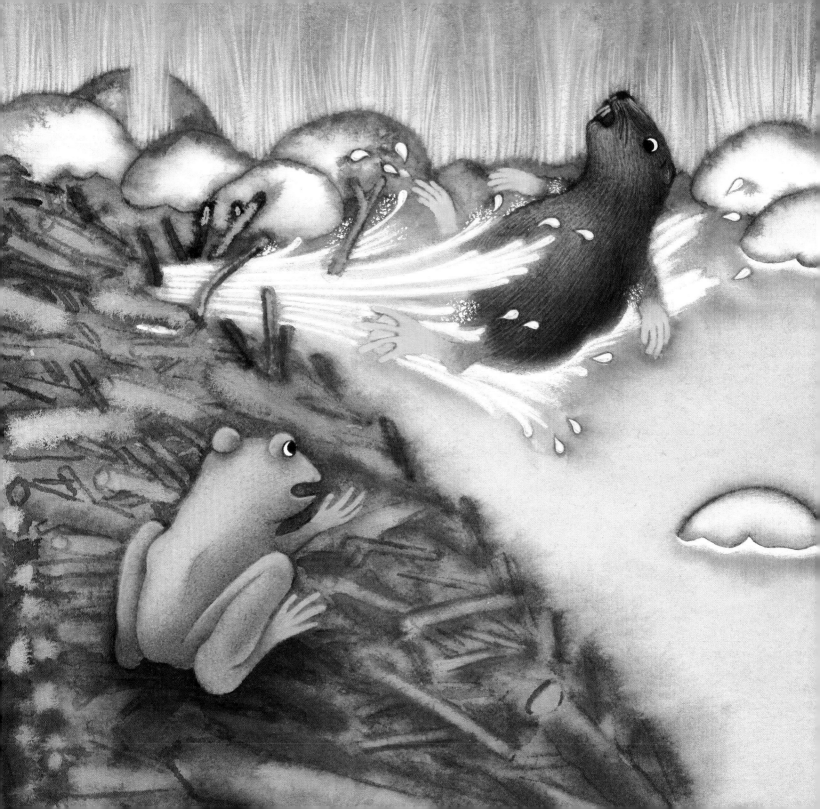

Boris was so startled that he even forgot to swim. But Freddy came to the rescue. With a mighty leap, he jumped down to the bottom of the stream and hauled the bewildered Boris back to the bank.

Father Beaver did an emergency repair job on the dam, and Mother Beaver said, "I think we've done enough work for today, don't you, Boris? Come and have supper with us, Freddy!"

Freddy was happy to accept the invitation. He swam off to the beavers' lodge with his three new friends. He thought it was really exciting to dive down to the underwater doorway and then come up into the lodge through the long passages.

Father Beaver, Boris and Freddy were sitting comfortably in a circle when Mother Beaver brought supper in. All of a sudden Freddy turned greener than ever. "You're not going to eat those damp roots and bits of wet bark, are you?" he said. Secretly, he had been hoping for a nice fat fly or at least a few little midges.

The beavers stared at him in surprise. "Why, we always eat roots and bark."

"Oh well, never mind," croaked the frog. "I'll just go and catch myself a bite to eat."

Boris went out with Freddy and climbed on the roof of the lodge.

"Good luck!" he called after Freddy.

"See you tomorrow," croaked Freddy happily, swimming to the bank.